© Publication: Penguin Random House South Africa (Pty) Ltd,
The Estuaries No 4, Oxbow Crescent, Century Avenue, Century City, 7441

www.penguinrandomhouse.co.za

© Text and illustrations by: Dino J. Martins 2021

Publisher: Nandi Lessing-Venter
Proofread by: Glenda Laity

Set in Playfair Display 12pt
Cover design by Linki Brand and Dino J. Martins
Layout and design by Linki Brand

Printed by ABC Press

First edition 2021

978 1 7763 5032 2 (printed book)
978 1 7763 5033 9 (ePub)

Helpful
Hannah Hippo

By Dino J. Martins

Penguin
Random House
South Africa

The morning sunlight streamed down from a crisp, clear blue sky. All along the banks of the Ewaso Nyiro River, birds and butterflies danced about. The warm rays of the sun were welcome after the cold, rainy night. While most creatures were busy bustling about, searching for food, building nests, or just chasing each other about, a family of hippos was sleeping in the sunshine.

On a gently sloping river bank, a family of hippos lay basking in the sun. Apart from the occasional grunt or flick of an ear, the hippos were lying still. Hannah Hippo lay snuggled up next to her mother. She was one of the youngest and smallest members of her family. Their contented bellies were full of delicious fresh grass from last nights' grazing. For a hippo, there's nothing better than lying about in the warm sunshine in the morning with a full belly. They were fat and shiny, lying in the sun.

Hannah was very happy, resting her head on one of her mother's fat, comfy legs. Just as she was dozing off again, Hannah Hippo felt something land on her back. It was Ollie the Oxpecker.

Ewaso Nyiro River

EQUATOR

Mount Kenya

KENYA

Mount Kilimanjaro

INDIAN OCEAN

TANZANIA

"Good morning, Hannah!"
chirped Ollie loudly.

"Good morning, Ollie,"
replied Hannah, yawning.

"Come, Hannah, come,
I want to show you something!"
said Ollie Oxpecker as he moved closer to Hannah's ears.

"Go away, Ollie," said Hannah, "I'm enjoying my nap."

"Hannah, Hannah, come on –
I want to show you something!"
urged Ollie, pecking at Hannah's ears.

"What is it?"
asked Hannah, flicking her ears at him.

"There is something strange stuck in the mud,"
he replied.

"Ooooh, something strange?"
asked Hannah, sitting up. Now she was interested. For, as hippos go, Hannah was
one of the most curious members of her whole family. She loved looking at things,
learning about them and exploring the world around her.

"Yes, come,
come let me
show you!"
screeched Ollie.

Ollie flew down to the edge of the river. Hannah, followed as fast as she could. The river flowed, steadily and silently. The water shimmered in the sunlight. Dragonflies danced and chased each other to and fro.

"I don't see anything strange," said Hannah.

"Look down there," said Ollie, pointing at a lump in the mud.

"That looks just like a lump of mud," said Hannah.

"No, no!" said Ollie. "Look and listen! I heard it crying earlier."

Hannah peered down at the lump of mud. Yes, it did look a bit strange, and, yes, it moved a little too. Then Hannah thought she heard a little voice crying out. She moved closer, as the voice was very, very soft.

"Help me, I'm stuck in the mud," squeaked the little voice.

"Hello, little one," said Hannah, and she pushed her nose into the mud and lifted up the talking lump.

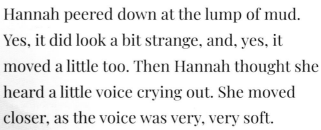

Freed from the mud, Hannah and Ollie
peered closely at the little creature. It had
a pointy beak, feathers, and large, bright
orange gangly feet.

"It's a little chick!"
exclaimed Ollie.

"Aaaw, you poor little thing," said Hannah, "How long have you been stuck in the mud?" she asked.

"I was swept away during the rain," cried the little chick. "Now I'm lost, and I don't know how to get back to my nest."

The little chick looked so helpless, cold, wet, and tired. It was shivering. Hannah could see that this little bird needed help finding its way back to its parents and nest. Hannah loved helping others. It made her feel warm and good, and that made her happy.

"Don't worry," said Hannah, "we are going to help you."

"We need to find out where your nest and parents are," said Ollie.

The little chick was completely lost. It could not remember where its parents and nest were along the river. Hannah saw how frightened the chick felt, so she gently lifted the little bird on her broad nose and lowered him into the edge of the water, so that they could wash the mud off his feathers. Then she carried him back up into the sunshine so that he could dry and warm up.

Now Hannah Hippo and Ollie Oxpecker had to figure out how they were going to help. There were lots of birds that lived along the river, so surely the chick must belong to one of those families.

They decided that first they would ask the Egyptian Geese who lived nearby.

Lifting the little chick onto her nose, and with Ollie perched on her back, Hannah walked down to the sandbank in the middle of the river where the Egyptian Geese lived. The nest was in a large old acacia tree-hollow, but now their chicks had left the nest and were often seen swimming alongside their parents.

As Hannah approached, the geese honked out loudly, "Hello Hannah! Are you coming to visit us?"

"Good morning, Mr. and Mrs. Goose!" said Hannah. "Are you, or anyone you know, missing a little chick?"

The geese gathered around, honking and hissing excitedly.

"My, oh my!" honked Mrs. Egyptian Goose.

"Can you count our goslings, Papa Goose?" honked Mrs. Egyptian Goose.

"All five goslings present and accounted for, my dear," he replied.

"Hannah, it appears that we have all of our chicks," said Mrs. Egyptian Goose.

"Well then, can you perhaps help us identify this little chick?" asked Hannah. "This little chick is lost and can't remember where his nest is."

The two Egyptian Geese waddled up and peered closely.

"My, oh my!" honked the Egyptian Geese, "That is a strange looking chick! It has such long toes!"

"I'm sorry," said Papa Goose, "but we don't recognise him. Perhaps you can ask our neighbours, the Blacksmith Plovers."

Hannah and Ollie thanked the Egyptian Geese and set off
towards where the Blacksmith Plovers lived. The Blacksmith
Plovers had made their home among some reeds growing
at the edge of the river in a quiet and peaceful spot from
which they ventured out each day.

As Hannah approached, with Ollie perched on
her back, and the little chick perched on her
nose, the Blacksmith Plovers stood up and
watched in amazement. Bobbing their
heads up and down in excitement,
the Blacksmith Plovers called out
to Hannah.

"Good morning, Hannah Hippo! Good morning, Ollie Oxpecker!" they called.

"Good morning, Mr. and Mrs. Plover," replied Hannah and Ollie.

Calling out with their distinctive, metallic cry, the Blacksmith Plovers ran to meet Hannah and Ollie. Hannah explained that they had found a lost chick and were trying to help him find his way back home. She asked the Plovers if they were missing a chick, but they said that they had just one chick, who was hidden safely in the reeds by the riverbank.

The Blacksmith Plovers could see how disappointed Hannah, Ollie and the little chick were.

"Now, now," clucked the plovers, "no need to be sad. We will see if we can help figure out how to get this little chick back home."

"I saw a lot of chicks walking past yesterday," said Mrs. Plover. "They were running after their family, the Vulturine Guineafowls".

"They will be back soon," said Mr. Plover. "Why don't you all rest here in the shade and wait for them?"

Hannah, Ollie and the little chick sat down to wait. The sun climbed higher and higher in the sky. The day grew warmer. Dragonflies and butterflies danced faster and faster around them.

A loud cackling noise could be heard in the distance, getting louder and louder.

Mrs. Plover called out to Hannah,
"The Vulturine Guineafowls are on their way!"

Hannah sat up. From a distance, a long line of Vulturine Guineafowls approached. She watched them and marvelled at their colourful spotted feathers and the brilliant blue bibs on their chests. The guineafowl moved swiftly down to the waters' edge, where they lowered their heads and started to drink from the river.

Hannah approached them slowly since she did not want to startle them.

"Excuse me, dear Vulturine Guineafowls," said Hannah. "Would you by any chance be missing one of your chicks?"

The guineafowls all turned around to look at her. They all started speaking at once, cackling and shrieking as loudly as they could. Hannah and Ollie tried repeating their question, but no one could hear them above the din. Then, the chief Vulturine Guineafowl came marching down.

He stood tall. His bright red eyes gleamed as he lifted up his head and shouted louder than anyone else, "What, what! What is all this noise about?"

The flock fell silent. Hannah approached a bit closer.

"I'm sorry to trouble you, but we were wondering whether you were missing one of your chicks," she said.

Chief Guineafowl cackled loudly and asked, "Well, young lady, why would you ask such a question? Why are you interrupting our water drinking? We are on a tight schedule, you know. What, what! Now, speak up!"

Hannah was a bit nervous talking to Chief Guineafowl, and was just thinking about how to best to explain when Ollie flew down and chipped in: "Hannah and I are trying to help a lost chick find his way home."

"Lost chick, you say?" cackled the guineafowl.

"Yes, we've asked the Egyptian Geese and the Blacksmith Plovers, who recommended we speak to you," said Hannah.

"Hmmmm, sounds a bit fishy, if you ask me," clucked Chief Guineafowl.

"We ARE trying to help this lost chick!" replied Hannah.

"Yes, Yes! They are trying to help a lost chick!" shrieked the Blacksmith Plovers, who had come running up to see what all the noise was about.

Hannah went on to explain to the guineafowl what had happened so far that day. She then fetched the little chick and placed him on the ground in front of all the guineafowls. They gathered around, peering closely. Whispering and gently prodding, they chattered away.

"Not one of ours! Not one of ours!" they cackled in unison. "Look! A guineafowl's feet are nothing like that!"

The Chief Guineafowl once again stood tall and shrieked louder than anyone else, and they all fell silent and bowed their heads.

"I'm sorry, but I am afraid that this is not one of our chicks," he said to Hannah, as kindly as he could. He pointed up at a thick clump of grass as a whole line of fluffy, speckled little guineafowl chicks emerged. "All present and accounted for?" called Chief Guineafowl.

"Yes, sir, all chicks present!" replied the flock.

Chief Guineafowl turned to Hannah and said, "I'm sorry, but we can't help you. As you can see, we have all our chicks. We don't recognise your little lost friend."

Hannah and Ollie looked down sadly. It seemed like they were never going to be able to find the lost chick's nest and reunite him with his family. Chief Guineafowl noticed how sad they were.

Despite being a very formal bird, he had a soft heart, so he decided to do what he could to help them.

"You are brave and kind," said Chief Guineafowl. "Let me see if I can help ask more creatures if they know who this lost chick belongs to."

With that, he flew up into a tall acacia tree and, at the top of his voice, called out to all that could hear. Now, guineafowls are very, very loud, and the loudest of all is Chief Guineafowl. So the message about the lost chick was told and told again, all along the river.

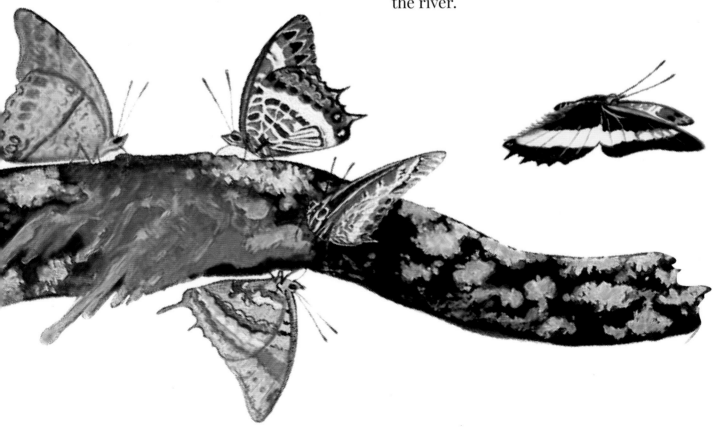

Hannah and Ollie settled down next to their
little friend and waited in the shade
until word had spread far and wide.

Many different creatures came by to see the
little lost chick.

Some Ants and Aardvarks.
Many Butterflies and Bushbabies.
A few Egrets and Elephants.
Several Hornbills and Hyrax.
A couple of Kingfishers and Kudus.
Two Otters and an Oryx.
A pair of Zebras and a Zorilla too!

Hannah and Ollie spoke to them one and all.
She asked again and again:

"Does anyone know who this
little chick belongs to?"

Sadly, no one seemed to be able to solve the puzzle of where the little chick came from. Hannah and Ollie waited and watched. Every time a new creature appeared, they leapt up, hopeful that finally it would solve the mystery.

But no one had an answer. No one seemed to know to whom this little chick belonged.

The day grew hotter as the afternoon wore on. Hannah decided to take a dip in the river to cool down. Hippos have very sensitive skin that needs to be kept cool and moist. Hannah waded into the water. As she settled down, the wonderful water flowed around her. It tickled her toes and made her skin feel good. She was just dozing off when she felt something tickling her nose.

Hannah opened her eyes and noticed a beautiful red dragonfly perched on her ear.

"Good afternoon, little dragonfly, I'm Hannah Hippo," she said.

"Good afternoon, Hannah, I'm Red Dropwing," buzzed the dragonfly.

Hannah smiled. She had a good feeling about this new friend she was making. Red Dropwing's voice was really, really soft, but he had something very, very important to say.

"I'm here to help you get the lost chick home," hummed the dragonfly. "I heard Chief Guineafowl shouting his message earlier as I was flying by. Every day, I travel up and down this river. I see many things. I hear many things. I learn many things..." whispered the dragonfly. "I know where the little lost chick's nest is!" he declared in the loudest little voice that he could manage.

The dragonfly went on to explain: "There was some heavy rain last night, and the river flooded. In a hidden bend in the river, there was a very special nest, woven by two rare, beautiful birds. This nest floated at the waters' edge. It was woven into a tangled bank, with a special secret entrance that was hidden in the water. This nest belonged to very special birds called Mr. and Mrs. Finfoot. As the water rose, the nest flooded, and the little chick was swept away. The baby Finfoot's parents have been searching for him," the dragonfly whispered sadly.

Hannah could barely contain her excitement.
She rushed out of the water and woke up Ollie
and the little chick, crying out excitedly:

"Wake up! Wake up! We've found
out where your nest is.
Red Dropwing, the dragonfly, just
told me... Come! Come!
Let's get you home!"

said Hannah, as she lowered her nose to let the chick
climb onto her head.

With Ollie flying alongside, she ran back down to the
river. The dragonfly was waiting for them.

"Follow me," he said. "I will show you how to
get to the Finfoot nest, but you are going to
have to swim up to the bend in the river."

"Lead the way," replied Hannah,
"I will carry the little chick
and follow you in the
water."

Red Dropwing Dragonfly flew up into the air. Ollie Oxpecker flew alongside and helped shout directions to Hannah Hippo as she swam. The little chick held onto Hannah's neck with his big orange toes. The dragonfly flew swiftly up the river. Hannah had to swim with all her might to keep up. Her short, fat legs paddled as fast they could. The current in the river was pretty strong for a small hippo. But Hannah was determined.

Hannah swam and swam.

She swam past the Blacksmith
Plovers, resting among the reeds.
She swam past the Egyptian Geese,
sunning themselves on the sandbank.
She swam past the other hippos,
asleep in the river.

Hannah Hippo kept swimming and
swimming until she reached the
bend in the river. Just as she thought
that she couldn't swim anymore, she
heard the dragonfly above her, call
out: "We're almost there!"

By the bend in the river, the trees
arched over the water and the
tangled bank was covered in creepers
and flowers all woven together. Red
Dropwing danced in the air above
them, and sang, "Let me see if I
can find the Finfoots!"

Deep in the tangled bank, Mr. and Mrs. Finfoot sat sadly, sighing, wondering if they were ever going to see their young one again.

The dragonfly fluttered between the flowers, calling out:

"Finfoots, Finfoots,
Don't be shy! Don't hide away!
Hannah Hippo is here to play!
She's brought a gift for you to see,
So come out now and dance with glee!"

Ever shy and secretive, the Finfoots peeked cautiously out from their tangled bank. What they saw made their hearts fill with joy. For there, clinging with all his might onto Hannah's head, using his giant orange feet, was their lost chick!

Singing with joy, Mr. and Mrs. Finfoot emerged from their hiding place.

"Our lost chick is back safely!" they cried out, as they greeted their little chick. The baby Finfoot danced about and climbed onto his dad's back. He settled down and sang out:

"Thank You! Thank You, Red Dropwing!"

"Thank You! Thank You, Ollie Oxpecker!"

"Thank You! Thank You, Hannah Hippo!"

Mr. and Mrs. Finfoot tilted their heads back and, in unison, sang a duet in honour of the three heroes. Hannah smiled, forgetting how tired she was. Ollie flew in happy circles, and the Red Dropwing danced with joy. The sun shimmered on the water. Hannah's little heart filled with joy. It felt so good to help someone. It was wonderful to see the baby chick reunited with his parents.

The sun was low in the sky, so now it was time for Hannah to return to her family. Hannah and Ollie said goodbye to the Finfoot family. The Red Dropwing dragonfly fluttered away among the flowers, singing softly to himself. Hannah floated back down the river. Ollie flew in circles above her, crying out,

"Hannah Hippo is a hero!
Hannah Hippo is a hero!"

All along the banks of the Ewaso Nyiro River, all the different creatures echoed his call:

"Hannah Hippo is a hero!
Hannah Hippo is a hero!"

Hannah floated back down the river to join her family.
Soon she was back snoozing in the setting sun, resting
her head on her mother's big, broad back. Tired from
her adventure and all the excitement,
Hannah Hippo fell fast asleep.

The End.